WELCOME TO
PASSPORT TO READING
A beginning reader's ticket to a brand-new world!

Every book in this program is designed to build read-along and read-alone skills, level by level, through engaging and enriching stories. As the reader turns each page, he or she will become more confident with new vocabulary, sight words, and comprehension.

These PASSPORT TO READING levels will help you choose the perfect book for every reader.

READING TOGETHER
Read short words in simple sentence structures together to begin a reader's journey.

READING OUT LOUD
Encourage developing readers to sound out words in more complex stories with simple vocabulary.

READING INDEPENDENTLY
Newly independent readers gain confidence reading more complex sentences with higher word counts.

READY TO READ MORE
Readers prepare for chapter books with fewer illustrations and longer paragraphs.

This book features sight words from the educator-supported Dolch Sight Words List. This encourages the reader to recognize commonly used vocabulary words, increasing reading speed and fluency.

For more information, please visit passporttoreadingbooks.com.

Enjoy the journey!

Cover design by Elaine Lopez-Levine

Little, Brown and Company
Hachette Book Group
1290 Avenue of the Americas, New York, NY 10104
Visit us at LBYR.com
mylittlepony.com

First Edition: June 2019

Little, Brown and Company is a division of Hachette Book Group, Inc.
The Little, Brown name and logo are trademarks of Hachette Book Group, Inc.

The publisher is not responsible for websites
(or their content) that are not owned by the publisher.

Library of Congress Control Number 2019937642

ISBNs: 978-0-316-42298-7 (pbk.), 978-0-316-42299-4 (ebook),
978-0-316-42297-0 (ebook), 978-0-316-42295-6 (ebook)

Printed in the United States of America

CW

10 9 8 7 6 5 4 3 2 1

Passport to Reading titles are leveled by independent reviewers applying the standards developed by Irene Fountas and Gay Su Pinnell in *Matching Books to Readers: Using Leveled Books in Guided Reading*, Heinemann, 1999.

Licensed By:

My Little Pony

RAINBOW ROADTRIP

Adapted by **Celeste Sisler**

Based on the screenplay

by **Kim Beyer-Johnson**

LITTLE, BROWN AND COMPANY

New York   Boston

Attention, My Little Pony fans!
Look for these words when you read this book. Can you spot them all?

balloon

rainbow

windmill

lumber

The town of Hope Hollow is
having a Rainbow Festival
for Rainbow Dash!

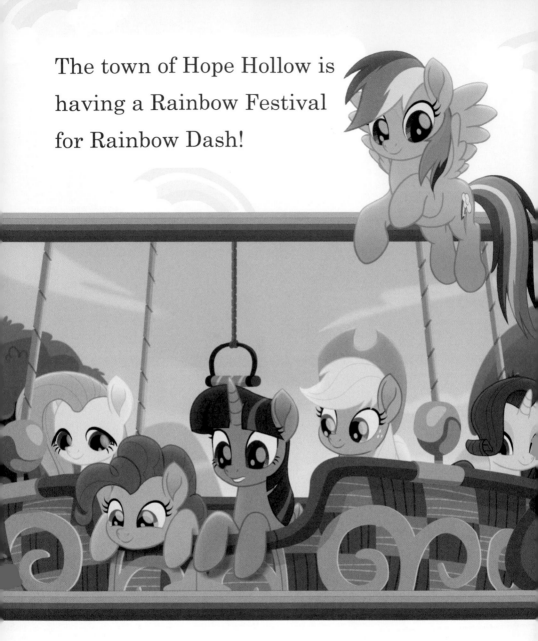

The Mane Six decide
to go on a road trip!

The ponies take a hot-air balloon to get to Hope Hollow.
WHOOSH!

They fly long into the night.
Pinkie Pie keeps watch while
her friends are asleep.

She sees a rainbow,
but she is not worried.
The ponies can fly through it!

CRASH!
That is NOT a rainbow.
It is a rainbow sign!

Uh-oh!
The balloon rips.
It falls through
the air!

Princess Twilight Sparkle
uses her magic.
She gets her friends
to the ground safely.

The Mane Six have
landed in Hope Hollow,
but they do not see
anypony to greet them.

They head into town.

"Look, there is somepony,"

Fluttershy says.

Her name is Petunia Petals.
She welcomes the ponies
to Hope Hollow.

Twilight notices that
Petunia is a little...gray.

The next day, the ponies explore.

Something is not right.

"Look around," Rarity says. The ponies see that there is no color in Hope Hollow. Everything is gray!

17

The ponies meet
Mayor Sunny Skies.

Twilight asks him why the town is gray.
The mayor avoids her question.
Instead he shows them...

...the outdoor spa...

...the butterfly
garden...

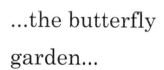

...and the famous
rainbow trout!

Rainbow Dash and
her friends are confused.
This does not seem like
a Rainbow Festival.

What is going on?
They try asking
Sunny Skies again.

"There is no
Rainbow Festival!"
the mayor shouts.
The ponies gasp.

The mayor tells everypony that
Hope Hollow used to be colorful.

All the townsponies
were friendly with
one another.

The mayor's grandpa even
built a rainbow generator.

But those happy days came to an end.
Ponies stopped being friendly.
The rainbow generator broke,
and the town lost its color!

That is why Sunny asked
Rainbow Dash to come
to Hope Hollow.

He thinks she can get
everypony excited again!

The Mane Six are happy to help!

Rainbow Dash sees two Pegasi in the sky.

Their names are Pickle and Barley, and they are brother and sister. Rainbow Dash is their favorite Wonderbolt!

Rainbow Dash gives Barley
and Pickle a flying lesson.

They are so excited!
Suddenly, a windmill
turns blue!

Rarity goes to a town shop.
She meets Kerfuffle, who
also makes clothes.

"I simply love your designs,
darling," Rarity tells Kerfuffle.
Suddenly, a hat turns purple!

PING!

Applejack helps fix the rainbow sign.

She admires the repairpony's talent.

Suddenly, the lumber turns brown!

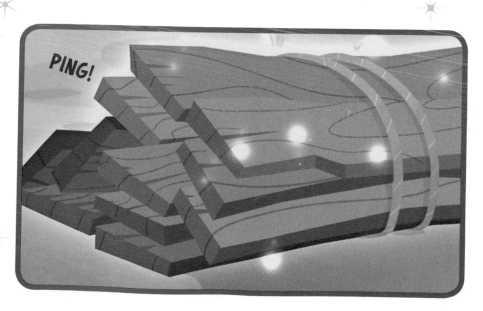

The ponies notice color
coming back all over town.
It did not go away because
the rainbow generator broke....

PING!

It went away because the ponies in Hope Hollow stopped being friendly! The Magic of Friendship and coming together has saved the day.

Mayor Sunny Skies
thanks the Mane Six.
Everypony in Hope Hollow
is excited again.

Let the most colorful
Rainbow Festival begin!